Wild Dolphin Rider

Wild Dolphin Rider

by Nancy Donovan
illustrated by Susan Spellman

Peter E. Randall Publisher

Portsmouth, New Hampshire

2015

Published by
Peter E. Randall Publisher
Box 4726
Portsmouth, NH 03801

www.perpublisher.com

Book design: Grace Peirce
www.nhmuse.com

To all my grandchildren and their generation who will be the next stewards of the Earth; especially to Sean, for whom this story was begun.

Contents

Appreciation

Pat Parnell for her continued support and editing; The Stratham Library Writers Group, who keep me revising; Wendy Lull, President of the Seacoast Science Center, Rye, New Hampshire, for reviewing an early version of this book; Ellen Goethel, PhD, for her advice; my grandsons, Stephen Donovan and Sean Okimoto, for their editing and suggestions.

Beginning the Journey

"Where the heck are the wild dolphins?" Sean complained. "I'm getting tired of sitting on these hard rocks. I've been waiting all summer to swim with them. The fishermen said they were here . . ."

Sean was sitting on the long rock jetty that stretched out from the shore to protect the boats in the harbor from storms. He'd been there since sunrise waiting for dolphins, and now the sun was making diamonds on the waves and no dolphins were in sight.

Yesterday, Sean had been hanging around the docks and heard the fishermen say they'd seen a pod of dolphins just outside the harbor entrance. One fisherman said a dolphin kept swimming beside his boat and clicking, as if trying to communicate. "Too bad I don't speak dolphin," the fisherman had chuckled.

"Hooray!" Sean had thought. "They're finally here. But I'm not going to wait for them to come into the harbor; I'm going to go out and meet them. Tomorrow morning I'll climb out on the far side of the jetty. I'll sit on the rocks at the very end and watch for the dolphins. When they come, I'll jump in the water and swim with them."

All last night Sean had dreamed of dolphins. In his dream, he was splashing and playing with them. He balanced on the tips of their beaks and they tossed him around like a ball in a dolphin show. He rode them like a surfer rides a board. And he talked with them!

When he'd woken up in the still-gray of early morning, he was sure today would be the day.

He'd left his house just after sunrise. His parents and his sister, Lauren, had still been asleep. He'd had a quick breakfast; pulled on his trunks, a beach shirt, and his baseball cap; and then grabbed a towel and filled his water bottle. He'd left his parents a note saying he'd be on the jetty. Then he'd slipped out of the house, closing the door quietly, and had run down the short lane to the harbor.

All the houses in the neighborhood were still dark. Not even the early morning runners were about yet. The birds were making their morning calls, but that was it. Sean smiled, "I feel like this whole morning is just for me. I know this will be the day the dolphins come."

At the jetty, the sun hadn't been up long enough to take away the night's chill. The rocks were cold and slippery. He slipped a couple of times on the seaweed that draped over them and scraped his knee on the barnacles. He'd done that before—no problem. He was in too much of a hurry to worry about it. "I'll wash it in the ocean later," he thought.

Now he was sitting on the very last rock. He could only wish and wait.

He saw the fishing boats leaving the harbor escorted by flocks of screaming gulls. The sounds of the boat motors rumbled across the water.

He smelled whiffs of seaweed, engine fumes and salt on the gusty wind.

He washed off his scraped knee.

He drank some water from his bottle.

And he waited.

"Where the heck are the dolphins? I've been here for at least an hour. These rocks are hard—the towel isn't much of a cushion. I know they'll come, if I just wish hard enough . . . "

"Maybe they don't know I'm here," Sean thought. He called, "*Hellooooo* dolphins—it's me, Sean. I want to swim with you." Yeah, like they'd really listen . . .

A breeze made the bay choppy. Sunlight slanting
on the waves made it hard to see whether anything was
swimming by. Sean pushed his straight brown hair out
of his eyes. Even with his baseball cap on, there was
too much glare.

He dangled his feet in the water. Suddenly he felt
something wet and smooth pressing against his leg—

he yanked his feet up. "What's that?" he yelped. Then he looked down. "Wow! A dolphin!"

The dolphin lifted its head out of the water, looked straight in Sean's eyes, and clicked.

Sean was so startled he forgot to jump in the sea the way he'd planned. He just stared at the dolphin. "You're a beautiful animal. And you're so big. You're almost as long as my mom's Mini Cooper car. You didn't seem so big in the marine park."

The dolphin was gray, sleek and smooth. It had a large, rounded forehead and a short, bottle-shaped beak that opened when it clicked. A high dorsal fin curved out of the middle of its back.

The dolphin continued its clicks. It looked as if it were smiling.

Sean said, "I wish I could understand dolphin so I'd know what you were saying."

He reached down and stroked the dolphin's cool, smooth skin. As he touched the dolphin, its gray color began fading to white. When the dolphin was white to its tail, the clicks turned into words in Sean's mind.

"Hello, Sean. I'm glad to meet you."

Sean's brown eyes popped wide open. "I can hear words in my mind—like you're talking to me. But you're still clicking. And how did you just turn white? And how do you know my name?"

"Sean, you called me. There are more ways of understanding than hearing things with your ears. As to why I now look white—it's my spirit talking with your spirit—what makes me, me, talking with what makes you, you. To everyone else I still look gray. My spirit could hear you calling out to see dolphins. And so I came. Why did you want to see me?"

"I want to know what dolphins are really like when they're free. Where they go—what they see. I want to explore what's out there—what's under the ocean, see what creatures live there," he said. "Dolphins seem friendly, not scary like sharks, and not as big as whales. They even try to play with fishing boats. I hoped I could make friends with them. Maybe they could take me to their secret places. They seem to swim everywhere, and they're always happy and playing.

"I feel sad for the dolphins in marine parks," Sean continued. "They can't like being penned in all the time. They always look like they're trying to communicate with us."

"You're right, Sean," the dolphin clicked. "Some of us have sacrificed freedom to work with humans. Others have been captured. We want people to understand that the oceans are beautiful, but they are dangerous and fragile. It's where a lot of creatures and plants live. It's our home."

Sean laughed. "Sure, it's beautiful and maybe dangerous, but it's sure not fragile. I've seen some pretty strong surf and storms. It's the shore that gets beaten up. The ocean does okay for itself."

"Maybe you need to see it from the ocean side, Sean. Storms aren't the only things that cause damage, to you or to us. Lots of stuff happens in the ocean. Would you like to swim with me for a while and see something of our world?"

"Would you take me? That would be great. I love swimming and bodysurfing in the big waves at the beach. Riding a dolphin would be the ultimate experience."

"The ocean is more than clear blue water and foaming waves," the dolphin clicked. "Underneath is a whole other world. It can be perilous, especially for outsiders. Are you really sure you're ready for this? I can't guarantee that I can bring you safely home."

"I've been waiting for this for years—let's go. It would be so great. I'd see things the way dolphins do . . . "

"Okay. Climb down on the rocks below the surface. When you're halfway in the water, straddle my back. Hold onto my fin and we'll glide out to the deeper ocean. As long as you touch me, you'll be able to hold your breath as long as I can when we dive.

My body will give you oxygen. Don't let go, whatever happens. You could drown."

Sean slipped into the cold water beside the dolphin. He reached out his arm and slid his hand around its dorsal fin. It took him just a moment to climb onto the dolphin. "Okay, I'm ready. Let's go."

Together they swam away from the rocks toward the open sea. Sean shivered—the water was cold, and he was also a little afraid. The shore was getting farther away awfully fast. Sean thought, "If I fall off now I'm in trouble. I'm too far out to swim back."

Screeching gulls were circling and diving so close to him, if he had reached up, he could probably have touched a wing. But he wasn't about to let go of the dolphin's fin.

"Hold on tight, Sean; we're going to practice diving and leaping. You won't be able to talk when we're under the surface. You have to remember to think what you want to say to me. You can only hear me in your mind—and I can hear you the same way in my mind."

Water rushed over them as they dove under the waves. Sean gripped the dolphin's fin as tight as he could. He could feel his legs slipping back toward the dolphin's tail.

"Whoa! I'm slipping . . . "

"Hold tight, get ready now for a leap . . . "

The dolphin pumped its flukes through the water. Suddenly Sean and the dolphin flew from the waves into the air in a perfect curve. Water sprayed off them, making tiny rainbows. They landed back in the water beak first and glided again beneath the waves.

"WOW! Take it easy, I need to get used to this. I almost fell off that time. And I lost my baseball cap. Can we take things a little slower? This isn't like the boogie boards and tubes I've practiced on."

"Sean, we can't do slow leaps. Hold on tight now, we're going to make a series of shallow leaps. Sometimes local fishing boats are close to the harbor entrance, and if they see us, they try to avoid hitting us."

"Can they see me if I wave as we swim by?"

"I'm not sure how the magic works—I haven't tried this before."

"You mean I'm the first dolphin-rider you've ever taken?"

"A few of my relatives have done this, but you're my first rider."

"Oh, great. Neither of us knows what we're doing."

"Don't worry about it. Dolphins have done this for centuries. It's perfectly safe—I think. I've seen others do it. No one has complained."

"Of course they couldn't complain, if they drowned."

"Yes, I guess you have a point . . . Look, we're way beyond the harbor. There weren't any boats in the channel today."

Sean sat up straight on the dolphin's back, arms circled around its dorsal fin. Looking around, he thought, "I'm on an adventure! The choppy waves look like they're laughing. The sky is bright blue with only a few pillow clouds. I'm riding a dolphin! What could be better? WHEE!!!"

"So," he asked the dolphin, "where are we going?"

"We're going to meet up with some of my pod in the ocean, about ten miles from here."

"How will you find them? There aren't any roads out there."

"This big round bump on my head sends the sound of my clicks in a focused line. An echo of what's out there bounces back to me. I can hear it through my jaws and my teeth. Then my brain makes the sound into a picture."

"That's weird. You hear through your teeth. What happens if you get a cavity—or a tooth ache . . . "

"Remember, Sean, we don't eat candy . . . "

"What about sugar kelp?"

"Sean, we're carnivores."

Finding the Pod

Sean stretched out as flat as he could against the dolphin's cool, smooth back. They went swimming, diving, and surfacing in graceful arcs. After the first few leaps, Sean got the hang of it and settled in for the ride. He noticed the ocean was calmer further from shore. Soft swells replaced the glittering spray of the choppy waves near the coast.

"What's your name? I want to call you something besides 'dolphin.' It could get awfully confusing when the other dolphins are with us."

"My family name is Delphinidae. My other name is Mari."

"Oh. You're a girl! So who's in your pod?"

"My mother, my two sisters, and our four calves."

"Are there any boys?"

"My son, Marius, is there. He'll stay with us for

another year. Females teach the calves to leap, dive and find good places to eat. When Marius is ready, he'll go off with the males. They protect us in the big pod. Sometimes the males join us for a while. We have strong group ties."

"Will I be able to understand the other dolphins the way I can hear you?"

"I think so—at least when we're close together. It may not work so well over long distances."

Sean's head was near Mari's blowhole. Just then she exhaled. He was showered with air and fine, wet spray. He shook his head and sputtered to clear the water from his eyes and nose. "That smells gross. You should have warned me that was coming."

"Sorry, Sean."

"Mari, I can hear clicks now. Is that the pod calling you?"

"Yes. There's some problem. We have to hurry to the pod now. Their clicks say it's urgent and they want to swim away from here right away."

"Okay. It's amazing! I can see the images you have of the shapes ahead of us."

"Hold on tight now, I'm going to dive and come up in the middle of them. They'll be surprised to see you. They didn't believe I was really going to get a boy-person."

Sean held his breath as he and Mari dove.

They surfaced in a rush of water. They were in the middle of the dolphin pod.

"Oh, Mari," someone clicked. "What have you done?'

All the dolphins seemed to be clicking at once. Clicks and words jumbled together in Sean's mind. The dolphins sounded angry.

"Who is with you?"

"Why did you bring him?"

Sean held tighter to Mari. He thought, "They're going to dump me off in the deep water . . . "

One of the dolphins made a series of clicks. To Sean, it sounded like, "Let Mari tell us."

The other dolphins quieted.

Mari clicked calmly, "I've brought Sean. His spirit was calling to me. He wants to get to know dolphins and see what's happening in the oceans. He's a friend."

Then one dolphin, who seemed to be the leader, clicked, "Hurry, Mari. We don't have time for touring. The tuna boats are coming. We have to swim away fast."

Dangerous Waters

CHAPTER 3

*M*ari and the other dolphins quickly surrounded the four calves. The largest calf cruised close to Mari's side. "Sean, this is Marius, my wonderful son."

Marius gently bumped his beak against Sean's leg. When Marius made contact and clicked, Sean could understand he was saying, "Hello."

Mari clicked, "Hold on tight. We're leaving at full speed."

Sean leaned along the dolphin's back. This time he turned away from her blowhole. One shower was enough!

The pod quickly headed up the coast. They hoped to outrun the tuna boats coming toward them.

The sun was beginning to climb, and Sean was

getting hotter. The cold spray showering him tingled on his skin and tasted salty on his lips. "This is it," he thought. "I'm traveling with a dolphin pod like I dreamed. I'm glad I've got this shirt on—at least I won't get sunburned."

"Mari, how do you know the ships are coming?" Sean asked her. "Even if they do, they're hunting tuna, not dolphins. Nobody hunts dolphins. There're laws against that. It even says 'dolphin-safe' on the cans of tuna my mom buys. Fishermen can go to jail, or pay big money for catching dolphins with tuna nets."

"Sean, the ocean is vast," said Mari. "We don't know where it's dangerous. Tuna nets have caught thousands of dolphins. Some people don't obey laws. Sometimes fishermen chase us, and our calves get left behind. Dolphins only know that tuna boats can be dangerous, so we swim away. When I was a young calf, my best friend was Tursi. We were in a pod off the coast south of here. We used to play with the other calves in our pod, leaping, tail-slapping and spinning. We had plenty of food. One day, a small group of us was exploring close to the shore. We heard engines and saw boats, but we didn't pay attention. We didn't think they concerned us.

"Suddenly they were upon us. There seemed to be boats and nets everywhere. We scattered and swam in panic. I made it into the clear. Tursi didn't. She got trapped in a net. I could hear her clicking and calling, but in all the confusion I couldn't find her. Then her calls stopped."

"Mari, what happened then? Did she get away?"

"No, Sean. She was trapped in the net too long. She drowned. When the tuna boats haul in the nets, if they find a dead dolphin, they just cut it up for shark bait. That's why members of our larger pod patrol the coast. They send us a signal when the tuna fleet leaves the harbor and tell us what direction the boats are traveling."

Sean and the dolphins raced through the ocean. There was no time for talking now. They wanted to get far away from the tuna boats. They leaped and splashed, leaped and splashed. They couldn't go as fast as he and Mari did coming out from the harbor—the calves weren't yet strong enough. But they were swimming fast.

He tried to look around when they leaped, but the time out of the water was short—just enough to catch a breath before diving again. All he could see was sky and never-ending ocean.

"Maybe this wasn't such a good idea," Sean thought. "We must be halfway to the other side of the world. What was I thinking? Getting home could be a problem. I really could drown—and nobody knows where I am. I don't even see any boats . . . "

The dolphin pod was spread out. Mari's mother was in the lead. Her two sisters were split on the sides. Mari and Sean were at the rear. The calves were in the middle.

After a while, Sean lost all sense of time. He settled into the dolphins' rhythm of glide and leap, glide and leap. "WOW!" he thought. "This is amazing. I'm heading into the great unknown riding a dolphin. No one will believe this!"

Suddenly, almost in mid-leap, Sean heard some rapid clicks and the pod slowed. They cruised on the surface. The sky was darkening, and there were great rolling swells on the ocean. Sean knew there was usually a storm coming when the waves rolled like that.

"Mari, the clicks from the other dolphins are getting louder. What's happening?"

"Hold on, Sean, we have to change direction. There's a ship up ahead that's mapping the ocean bottom with sound probes. The sound can confuse our sense of direction."

The lead dolphin, Mari's mother, began to swim a zigzag course. One of the other dolphins leaped. They collided. The dolphin calves began to click and swim in circles. Mari and her sisters tried to gather the calves together. But the calves were panicking—splashing and clicking frantically.

Then Sean heard it—a booming sound that vibrated through his whole body. Mari began to twist and shudder. All the dolphins were now swimming wildly in all directions. Sean felt his hands slipping off Mari's dorsal fin. Desperately he squeezed his knees tightly against her sides.

He felt Mari trembling. His own heart was galloping. Dolphins were leaping and crashing all around him. He was buffeted by bodies and water. He couldn't tell where anyone was. The frenzy seemed to go on forever. It was all he could do to hold on to Mari as tightly as he could and hope it would stop soon.

Suddenly Mari dove deeper than Sean had been before. He could feel his heart racing, and his lungs seemed on fire. Then, just as fast as they had plummeted down, they were surging upward. With a mighty pump of her flukes, Mari leapt clear of the waves.

Sean felt his lungs taking in air in a great *whoosh*. Mari lay on the surface. Shudders moved through her great body. Sean lay limply across her back, his fingers barely able to clutch her dorsal fin.

Mari began calling, "Marius—Marius! Where are you?"

"Mari, what happened?"

Mari's reply filtered slowly into Sean's brain, "The sounds scrambled our directional systems. We had to escape it. The pod has scattered. I've lost my son."

Tuna Fleet

CHAPTER 4

Sean looked around the now-empty ocean. The waves were getting higher. There were no dorsal fins and no splashes in sight.

Mari began swimming in circles and sending out clicks. "Maybe he isn't too far away . . . "

Then her clicks bounced back from the north. A shape was far ahead, but it definitely was a dolphin. She swam straight toward it. More shapes were coming into view. There were three dolphins swimming together. Mari went as fast as her powerful flukes could propel her.

Once again Sean was speeding through the waves riding the dolphin—holding on as tight as he could. He thought, "This is not at all like riding a boogie board at the beach."

As the gap closed between the dolphins, Mari slowed. "It's not Marius. It's my mother and one sister. The calf with them is female . . . Marius isn't with them."

Sean heard clicks of conversation between Mari and the other dolphins. "What's happening?" he asked.

"My mother is leading them to a safe harbor. My other sister is searching for the calves. My mother thinks they may have gone in a different direction—Sean, we have to go back, where the tuna fleet is. I have to find Marius. I'm sorry. If we get caught in the nets, you could drown, too."

"Mari, I know we have to rescue Marius, no matter what. I thought dolphins just had fun splashing and diving and tail-walking—like in shows. I didn't think about life in the ocean being really dangerous. But we have to do whatever it takes. He's your son."

"Hold on, Sean, I'll be swimming as fast as I can. I hope he sends out location calls . . . "

Mari, with Sean stretched out along her back, both his arms wrapped around her dorsal fin, sped along the surface back toward the fleet. The ocean became stormier the further they swam.

Every so often they would stop. Mari would swim in widening circles, sending out her clicks. Images returned of small boats and, sometimes, floating

debris. Several times large ship images would return. Mari said those were tourist boats.

Once, Sean saw a huge ship, long and low in the water except for what looked like a house on the end of it.

"What's that ship, Mari? It doesn't look like a tourist ship."

"That's a tanker carrying oil. Look behind it. You can make out several more. We're close to the shipping lanes. We have to avoid those ships—their propellers are sharp. Even whales get injured."

They continued their desperate search.

The weather kept getting stormier. Soon the wind was blowing like a hurricane. Ominous dark clouds billowed on the horizon. The wind was churning up waves higher than Sean had ever seen. They towered over him, their tops curling down on him like the hands of an angry sea monster.

He and Mari crested huge swells, dropped down

into troughs between them and then rode up the next wave. Water swept over them in freezing torrents. Sean clung to Mari. His heart was beating fast and his body was shaking. This wasn't the tour of dolphin life he expected. This was real danger.

"Sean, we're going to dive to where the water is calmer. Those clouds may have lightning in them."

Just then, there was a blinding flash and a loud cracking sound. Sean screamed. Mari plunged below the waves.

Sean held on to Mari with all his strength. He didn't want to hear another sound like that crack. He couldn't ever remember a lightning flash that was so close to him. He was really glad to get below the waves where it was calmer. Stretched out on Mari's back, he could absorb warmth from her body. Every time they surfaced to breathe, he was frozen again, and he was afraid of the lightning.

For the first time since his adventure began, Sean thought of home. His parents would be worried when they didn't find him on the jetty where he'd said he would be. They were probably looking for him now.

"I didn't mean to worry them," he thought. "I just didn't think—think about how long I'd be gone or about telling someone I was going away with a dolphin . . . It all happened so fast. Maybe they'll think I've been kidnapped. Maybe they're crying. Maybe they think I drowned and are looking for my body. And my sister—she'll be looking under the jetty rocks."

He thought Lauren would believe he was playing a trick on her. He imagined her saying, "That's enough, Sean. Stop teasing us. It's not funny, Sean. Mom and Dad are in a panic. I know you're hiding somewhere."

He had no way to tell them where he was. No matter how loud he yelled, they couldn't hear him. He didn't have a cell phone. What if he did get caught in the tuna nets; would he be cut up for bait, too?

"Mari, we have to hurry," he said suddenly. "Why do you keep circling? It slows us down."

"I go as far as my calls can reach to the edge of one circle, then I go forward again, so my next circle will overlap the previous one. If Marius has gone this way, we should find him soon. He can't swim as fast as I can."

They continued their search through the stormy ocean. Battered and frozen, Sean clung to Mari. He kept thinking about his parents searching for him. "I bet my mom is worried. I hope they found my note. They'll find the towel and water bottle and know I was there. Oh, oh. If they find my cap floating, they'll really think I've drowned."

"Sean, this is terrible," Mari cried. "The tuna

fleet is in range of my clicks. I don't see Marius. Marius, where are you?"

Mari was clicking frantically, turning in all directions. "Marius . . . Marius . . . "

Then they heard it. Clicks weren't coming from the direction of the tuna fleet; they were coming from the shipping lanes where the tankers were.

Mari turned quickly and followed the clicks. The storm was less violent as they swam in a new direction.

Soon not just one dolphin shape emerged, but four. It was Marius, two female calves and Mari's sister. She had been searching, too, and had swum to the mid-ocean when Mari swam south. All were safe.

Marius swam quickly to Mari's side. "Hi, Mom. We escaped the loud noise. I led the other calves to safety. I protected them!"

"Oh, Marius, I was so worried. The next time you 'protect' someone, please send out location calls."

"Oh, yeah. I forgot."

"Yeah," Sean thought, "I forgot too."

Dolphin Games

CHAPTER 5

*T*he dolphins turned toward land. The storm was blowing away from them.

Marius kept bumping and rubbing Mari's side. Sean could hear Marius complaining, "Mom, I'm hungry—all that swimming sure builds up an appetite. When can we eat?"

"Marius, a little patience, please."

Sean thought, "I'm hungry, too, but I don't think I want to eat raw fish or squid or crunch lobsters. I'll just wait 'til I get home, whenever that is."

"Mari, why are we heading back to shore?" he asked.

"We're all exhausted and hungry. We want to go back to shallower water to feed. The calves won't need to dive so deep to get food. We can find fish, lobsters and crabs nearer the off-shore ledges."

"But, Mari, I thought there were more fishing nets around the shore, and with all the trawlers there, isn't that dangerous too?'

"Yes. It's all dangerous. Those are gill nets. We can get trapped in them. But some fishermen put alarms that make a pinging sound on them to warn us. The most terrible nets are the great free-floating drift nets lost in the deep ocean. There aren't any boats around them to give us warning."

The small group swam farther away from the shipping lanes. They moved past the storm. The ocean was settling down. Sean could hear thunder in the distance, but there were no more lightning strikes. The dark, mountainous clouds were behind them. The sky above them was blue once again.

Mari and the other dolphins swam across the ocean in smooth, graceful leaps. Sean sat up straighter on Mari's back—riding like a cowboy—yelling "Yahoo!" Shining spray streamed off him each time they surfaced. "Hey, I'm King Neptune, ruler of the oceans . . . "

It was becoming fun again, now that the calves were safe.

He thought, "I wish I had a video camera. No one

is going to believe me about this ride . . . "

Mari clicked, "Can you hear those new clicks? My mother and the others are joining us. We're close to the off-shore ledges."

He looked around to his left and saw a cluster of splashes moving in a line toward his group. "Now I see them—off to the left."

Mari warned him, "Be ready for lots of diving. We're in fishing mode. It's time to start looking for good feeding spots. You can listen to our sound waves at work. We're looking for rocky bottoms where lobsters hide, and vegetation where fish congregate."

The dolphin group spread out and sent clicks and whistles as they advanced.

Mari clicked, "Get ready . . . "

Sean felt colder water rushing over him as they dove. He could hear Mari's heart rate slow. Her flukes and pectoral fins stopped moving. It was like riding a torpedo. Sean saw bubbles rising around them. Stillness enveloped them as they plunged deeper.

Ahead, in the dim light, he could make out the ocean bottom littered with rocks. It looked like a boulder field that collapsed from a mountain. Rocks were jumbled across the ocean floor as far as he could see. Mari and the other dolphins leveled off their swim and began cruising parallel to the sea bed.

The older dolphins were nudging the calves, showing them how to look between and under rocks for lobster and crabs. Marius swam close to Sean and Mari. He was almost full grown. It was clear he'd done this before and didn't need much help getting his food.

Mari used her beak to root around the rocks. Sean could hear crunching, but from his position on her back, he couldn't see the unfortunate creatures she was having for lunch.

As if on a signal, all the dolphins turned, and with pumps of their flukes, surged up to the surface. Mari cleared the water and leapt into bright sunlight. Sean gasped as they broke through the waves. The ride was exhilarating. For a few seconds the light was blinding; then Sean and Mari crashed back into the waves with a mighty splash.

The pod was playful now, after the success of the hunt. The adults were doing spins in the air with their leaps. The calves were fluke-splashing and chasing each other around the pod.

Marius tried a double spin. He almost made it. Mari said, "Hold on, Sean. I want to give him a lesson in spinning."

Mari picked up speed, leaped into the air and did a double spin. She twisted so fast, Sean's hands slipped off her fin. In a flash, he landed on his back in the water.

Before he swallowed more than a mouthful, one of the other dolphins glided beside him. She put her beak under water and picked him up on her head.

"Whoa!" Sean yelled. "That was a surprise. I can swim, but I'm sure glad you picked me up. One swallow of salt water is enough."

Mari swam over and picked him up. "Sorry about that. I'll stick to single spins while you're my rider."

"That's a relief. Tell Marius I'm sorry for spoiling his lesson."

"There will be more time for playing with him after I bring you home."

Marius swam over to Sean. He touched his beak to Sean's leg and Sean heard him say, "Do you want to play with us? I'll give you a ride and spin, and my friends and I can show you some dolphin games."

"Great. That would be fun."

Sean stretched his arm across to Marius's fin and slid across from Mari's back.

"Here we go," Marius clicked. "We're playing 'touch-the-dolphin,' and I'm IT."

The three female calves swam in circles around Marius and Sean, clicking loudly. Sean knew right away the sounds meant "You can't catch me . . . "

Marius, with Sean aboard, made lunges and twists. Finally, he dove below the waves and suddenly came up outside the circle and surprised one of the other calves. There was much clicking and fluke splashing. In all the commotion, Sean fell off. He sputtered and called, "Mari, help!"

Mari slid under him and he settled again on her back. The dolphins continued their leaps and tail-walking for a short time, then they grouped together.

Sean asked Mari, "What's happening now?"

"We're going closer to shore. There's a bay we want to explore. It's where we were heading before the tuna boats and the sound probes threatened us. We need new fishing grounds. The fish stock in some of our old feeding grounds is disappearing."

"Where is it going?"

"Much of it is just dying. We don't know why. Some dolphins noticed there were a lot more plants growing in those areas. But that didn't concern us

at first. Then we noticed there weren't as many fish around. We don't know what caused it. It seems to follow a pattern. Lots of vegetation; fewer fish; plants die; no fish. Then it's a dead zone."

Sean asked, "Does it happen everywhere?"

"No. Mostly in those places where there are lots of people. There are many coves and river outlets where the fish can't survive anymore."

"Mari, what makes the vegetation grow so thick?"

"Sean, a lot of groundwater that the rain washes into the ocean tastes bad. We wonder what people are putting in it. And all kinds of nasty wastes come out of big pipes that empty into the ocean in places where lots of people live. Wherever the rivers and pipes empty into the ocean, it seems to make the vegetation overgrow."

"Mari, those bad-tasting things people spread on the land are chemicals to make our plant foods grow more. Maybe they make the ocean plants grow more, too. The big waste pipes carry all our garbage and poop into the ocean. I guess that would be pretty nasty."

"There are other things, too, Sean. In some places a black, sticky stuff gets on the feathers of birds and the fur of seals and otters. Many of them die. The water where lots of people live close to the shore gets a

41

shiny surface on big floating patches. We breathe it in through our blowholes. It irritates our skin."

"Mari, the sticky stuff is probably oil leaking from the tankers. The stuff that irritates your skin must be gasoline from roads and parking lots. Don't the fishermen complain that it's killing the fish?"

"Some fishermen are part of the problem, Sean. They keep catching more and more fish. Many of the ones they catch in nets, they don't even want. They throw them back dead into the sea. When they catch so many small fish, then the big fish and mammals like me can't get enough to eat. Also, some fish are contaminated with something. When we eat those fish, they can cause our calves to be born with problems."

"That's terrible, Mari. We could run out of fish. It would be awful to have an ocean with only dead critters in it. I wouldn't want to even swim in it. Maybe the oceans and critters in it aren't as strong as I thought. If all these things happen to them, then maybe people can damage the ocean. And if the ocean got damaged, what would happen to people?"

The dolphins and Sean continued cruising through the calm, blue water. He watched their graceful leaps and perfectly curved dives. Rainbows formed in the splashes. He knew he was the only person in this glorious, peaceful world. He thought, "I am so lucky. I wish everyone could see how beautiful this is."

On one of the dolphin's leaps, Sean saw a long line of high rocks not so far away. "Mari, I can see the shore up ahead."

"That's where the bay is we want to explore. It's not as close to people as our former fishing ground. The pod is hoping there isn't too much destruction."

After cruising just a little longer, Mari said, "Hold on tight; we're going to dive again."

As Sean, Mari and the pod descended, the water was clear. He saw waving seaweed, a kelp bed that looked like trees in a forest bending in the wind. Small schools of silvery fish darted in all directions. They seemed to be following a leader, first sweeping in one direction, then on some signal, reversing course. Other fish were round; some had bright stripes; others were pencil-thin.

"Mari, this is amazing. I didn't know it would be so beautiful—an underwater fairyland. I wish everyone could see this."

The dolphins cruised through the schools of fish, happily having an after-lunch snack. When the dolphins surfaced, there was much excited clicking.

"So, Mari, is this a good spot?"

"Oh yes. Everyone is relieved. We'll send a

message back to the large pod that we've found a good feeding place.

"Now it's time to bring you back to your jetty. Hold tight for the fastest ride of your life."

Sean clung to Mari as she leaped and cruised. Water streamed in glistening waves over boy and dolphin. Sean shouted, "This feels like flying through the ocean!"

Mari clicked, "We'll make one more stop on the way back. I want you to see a coral reef."

"Will there be colorful anemones? The ones I've seen in aquariums look like flower gardens. There are always unusual small fish around them—like butterflies in a garden."

"Wait and see, Sean. Some things are not as we imagine—or as they should be."

The pair continued their smooth ride through the calm ocean.

Without warning, Mari breached and did a double twist in the air. Sean lost his grip, and tumbled off her back.

He flailed and kicked trying to get to the surface, but he was falling faster than he could swim up. He tried to yell for help—but water filled his eyes, ears and mouth. He knew he could only get oxygen by touching Mari. He felt his heart pounding, and he imagined falling into a bottomless well where no one would ever find him. He was drowning.

Then Mari swept under him and caught him on her back.

"I couldn't breathe—I was drowning. Why did you do that, Mari?"

"I'm sorry I frightened you, Sean. I wanted you to understand how it is for marine creatures when the water loses oxygen. It feels like they're drowning, and sometimes they do. Look below. We're close to the reef now."

"What reef? I only see ridges of white, jagged

rocky stuff through this murky water."

"That white rocky ledge was a reef made by millions of tiny coral animals. It used to have the colorful anemones you saw in aquariums and lots of glittering fish. But plants covered the coral, and other chemicals came. The coral animals were suffocated by the vegetation. The reef died, the anemones died, and the fish have fled."

As they surfaced again through the murky water, they heard dolphin whistles and clicks.

Mari frantically clicked back, "We're coming . . ."

"What's the matter, Mari?"

"It's my son. He's trapped in a floating net . . . "

Spider Webs in the Ocean

CHAPTER 6

*M*ari, with Sean clinging to her, followed the path of the clicks at top speed. They headed toward the deeper ocean. Even at top speed, they seemed to be slow. Time froze. It was taking forever to find Marius.

Then they saw the net. Large fish Sean couldn't name were trapped. They hung suspended in the water. They weren't swimming, they were just hanging there. He thought, "Those fish look chewed up—like sharks or something have been eating them. This is awful."

He saw an enormous sea turtle. The net was caught under its shell. It wasn't moving. Sean knew it was dead.

"No wonder the dolphins are so afraid of

the floating nets," Sean thought. "They can trap anything."

And still they didn't see Marius. Sean could feel his own heart racing. This net seemed to go on forever. He wanted to shout for Marius, but he couldn't. Mari kept sending calls as they raced.

Then they saw him.

Marius was thrashing desperately to get free of the net.

Mari rushed to him. "Stop struggling. It uses up too much oxygen."

Sean saw the net had twisted around Marius's head and caught on his left pectoral fin.

Mari pushed her beak against the rope, trying to move it away, but it was too tight.

"Help, Mom, help! I can't get out. It hurts my fin. I didn't see it."

Mari dove under her son. She tried to lift him and the net above water so he could breathe. She managed to get him to the surface for just a moment. He took a quick breath. But the net was too big and too heavy with the weight of water and all the trapped creatures. She couldn't hold him there. The net dragged him under again.

Mari and Marius were getting desperate. Mari used her beak to try to push the net from Marius's fin. It just wouldn't move.

"Mari," Sean cried, "let me climb on Marius. Maybe I can move the net off his fin."

"Sean, if I can't do that, how can you . . . "

"Mari, just let me try. My fingers are strong. Maybe I can push the net to where the fin is narrower. That would make the rope looser. Then you could push it off. We have to do something . . . "

Mari leaned against Marius. Sean grabbed Marius's dorsal fin and stretched his leg to try to transfer across the dolphins.

He slipped and tumbled off both dolphins into the cold blackness.

In a second, Sean couldn't see Mari or Marius, or even light. He was falling into a void. He tried to scream for help and water filled his mouth. He could feel himself tumbling into the bottomless deep. The

water was too heavy for him to even move his arms
. . . then he crashed onto a solid cold surface.

It took Mari a minute to realize what had
happened. At first she thought Sean had transferred
to Marius. When she realized he had fallen, she
torpedoed down. Sean was flailing and kicking in his
attempt to surface.

Sweeping under him, Mari caught him on her
back. She raced to the surface with him. Sean clung to
her, throwing up water and gasping air.

"That was too close!" Sean said. "I was beginning
to panic—I was afraid you didn't notice I fell off. We
have to try again."

This time when they tried the transfer, Marius
was very still. His clicks were getting farther apart . . .

"Hurry, Sean. He's fading."

This time, Sean slipped across Marius's back
without a problem. He leaned over Marius's side and
tried to roll the rope to the narrower edge of the fin.
His fingers were stiff with cold. It was hard to wiggle
them under the net. Finally, it moved a little but not
enough. Sean was getting short of breath. Mari didn't
have much oxygen left to share. Sean would have to
find another way to move the rope.

Sean pulled hard against the fin. It was a little
flexible. He could pull it closer to Marius's body. The

pressure from his hands dented it just enough to let him roll the rope a little toward the end of the fin.

Mari was right beside the fin, watching. When she saw the rope move, she pushed her beak against the fin, denting it more. Sean pulled the net again closer to the end of the fin. They worked together—dent and pull—dent and pull. Finally the net slipped off Marius's fin. He was barely moving.

Mari swam under him and used her head to free him. Then she pushed him to the surface. Marius and Sean broke through the waves into fresh air. Sean gasped and took a deep breath. Marius shuddered; spray burst from his blowhole.

He was saved.

"Mom, I'm sorry. I just wanted to explore on my own. I didn't see the net."

"The main thing is, you're all right. It's time we brought Sean home. There has been enough excitement and adventure for one day. You owe your life to Sean."

"Thanks, Sean. I won't forget you. I'll always be your friend. If you ever need help in the ocean, call me."

Coming Home

CHAPTER 7

The two dolphins and Sean headed landward. They swam slowly. It would be awhile before Marius regained his strength.

They were so far out in the ocean, it would be a long ride to get to the shore. They cruised through gentle swells. The waves seemed to be helping them swim home.

Finally, Sean could see land in the distance. "I'm almost home," he thought. "How am I ever going to explain this to my parents? I went for a ride on a dolphin . . . "

Sean felt the water rippling over his back as the three of them headed to the jetty.

The entrance of the harbor was crowded with

boats of all sizes. Sean sat up straight on Mari's back. He held onto her dorsal fin with one hand and waved happily to the people in the boats. A great cheer went up from the closest boats. The cheer passed back to those closer to the shore. Sean saw a crowd gathering and running toward the jetty.

Standing on the end of the jetty were his parents and his sister.

As they approached the jetty, Mari clicked to Sean, "I'll swim up to the rocks where you climbed on my back. Be careful when you slide off. Grab onto the rocks."

"Oh, Mari. I don't want to leave you yet. There is so much more I want to see. I didn't know there was so much happening in the ocean. I didn't understand how things we do on land affect so many creatures. Will you come back?"

"Sean, Marius and I have to rejoin the pod. It's time for us to go. Hurry now. Climb on the rocks."

Sean scrambled to the top of the jetty. His parents hugged him tightly. Lauren said, "That was not a good trick, Sean. Everyone has been looking for you. I was scared you were drowned."

After a long family hug, Sean stood back from his parents. "I'm okay. I'm not hurt. I'm sorry I worried everyone. I've seen so many things in the ocean. Lots

of creatures live there. We need to take care of it—it could die."

Sean turned back toward the water. He waved with both arms to the dolphins and called, "Goodbye. Thank you. Please come back and take me again."

Mari clicked rapidly, but Sean could no longer understand what she was saying.

Marius breached, turned and did a tail-walk. Looking back at Sean, he nodded his head several times and sent a series of clicks.

Sean watched as the two dolphins, both gray now, leaped and dove playfully among the fishing boats until they reached open water and disappeared.

The bay turned golden in the last rays of the sun before it dropped below the horizon. Sean and his family turned for home.

Back on solid ground, Sean ran ahead, jumping with excitement. "Boy, have I had the best adventure of all time. I've made friends with wild dolphins! I knew I could do it! And I've been places in the ocean where nobody else has gone. I'll never forget today!

"Hey, Mom, what's for dinner? I'm starved."

Things to Know about Dolphins

Mari Answers Questions

How long have dolphins existed?

The current families of whales, dolphins and porpoises became established about five million years ago. They evolved from land animals millions of years before that.

If they started out as land animals, why don't they have arms and legs?

When they lived on land, they did have limbs. Pectoral fins or flippers closely resemble an arm with hands and fingers. Remains of pelvic bones that held their legs are found deep in their bodies. Those limbs gradually diminished as they evolved into marine creatures. Limbs would have been a hindrance to swimming and served no helpful purpose.

How many species are there?

There are thirty-four species of ocean dolphin and five species of river dolphin. There are more than eighty recognized species of whale, dolphin and porpoise.

If they're animals, why don't they get cold living in the ocean?

Blubber, a thick layer of insulating fat under the skin, provides protection. They need this because water pulls heat out of mammals twenty-five times faster than air does.

How often do dolphins breathe?

They breathe two to six times a minute.

How long can they hold their breath?

Generally about ten minutes—possibly longer in some conditions.

What happens when they dive?

When dolphins dive, the rib cage contracts, heart rate drops to about twelve beats per minute, and muscle activity decreases. Their lungs retain 80% of the oxygen they breathe in the air. Also, sponge-like cells in the blubber called "retia mirabilia" hold oxygen. This oxygen is then released into the blood when they are below the surface.

Do dolphins get "the bends" like divers do?

The "bends" is caused by nitrogen bubbles in the blood. Oxygen tanks used by scuba divers allow nitrogen to build up in their blood. This is not a problem for dolphins. Dolphins only breathe air on the surface. They use that reserved air when they dive.

How fast do dolphins' hearts beat?

During fast swimming, a dolphin's heart beats about 180 times per minute. It slows to about twelve beats per minute in a deep dive.

How long do they live?

Life expectancy is usually less than twenty years but may reach to forty years in captivity. It is not known for certain how long they live in the wild.

How do you tell how old a dolphin is?

Age is counted by growth rings or layers in teeth. A dolphin has only one set of teeth in its lifetime.

How do dolphins sleep?

They take short naps on or just below the surface. Only half the brain sleeps at a time. Dolphins are voluntary breathers. They have to maintain some consciousness to remember to breathe. They switch off one half of their brain at a time to get rest. In captivity, they may develop a tail reflex that keeps them in position with their blowholes above the surface.

How do they navigate over such long distances?

It is thought they may use geomagnetism—reading the Earth's magnetic field to navigate.

Why do they make those clicking sounds?

Dolphins use clicks for echolocation. Clicks are produced in nasal plugs on or in the larynx. The clicks are focused in a directional beam by the fatty "melon," the dolphins' rounded forehead. Return sounds are picked up by an oil reservoir in the lower jaw and transmitted to the brain as pictures. Teeth are somehow involved in this, too.

What is echolocation?

It's a way of seeing things beyond the range of eyesight. It uses the bounce-back or echo from a sound striking an object to identify it. Bats use a similar system. People use sonar for the same reason.

How can they hear sounds over miles of ocean that we don't hear?

Dolphins are able to hear many more frequencies that humans. Sound travels five times faster through water than through air

Can they recognize their own calves, or their friends?

It is believed that each dolphin has a signature whistle. It's like a name. Mothers teach their calves the whistles.

What do they eat?

Dolphins are carnivores. They eat crabs, lobsters, squid, fish and other prey.

How do dolphins swimming in the salty ocean get fresh water to drink?

They get most of their fresh water from the fish they eat. Some water is also in the fat they metabolize. Their kidneys are really good at retaining water.

Do they move faster in the air or in the water?

They move faster in the air. There is less resistance, or friction, in air than in water.

What are threats to dolphins?

Most threats to dolphins are human-made:

◆ Entanglements in fishing nets
◆ Pollution
◆ Habitat destruction
◆ Hunting and whaling
◆ Sound pollution
◆ Human disturbance
◆ Dead zones
◆ Large sharks are their natural predators

Why don't dolphins get those growths or barnacles on their heads like whales do?

Dolphins have remarkable skin. An entire layer of skin can be replaced in two hours. They also secrete a special gel that resists the attachment of barnacles.

Dolphin Facts

Bottlenose Dolphin Description

Breeding – Every 3–6 years

Calf weight at birth – 35–65 pounds

Calves nurse – 12–18 months

Clicking – Up to 1,000 clicks a second

Color – Shades of gray and white most common, helps with camouflage

Depth – Can reach 1,800 feet, but do not commonly go that deep

Diving – Holding breath, three to four minutes in-shore; about seven minutes in deep ocean, possibly longer

Dorsal fin – Curved or hooked

Gestation – Pregnancy lasts 12 months. Stay with mother up to 3 years

Life span – About 20 to 40 years in captivity. Uncertain, but maybe 15 to 30 years in the wild

Live calves – Born tail first underwater, pushed to surface by mother

Maximum length – 12-and-a-half-feet long

Maximum weight – 1,435 pounds

Prominent forehead – Melon

Reproductive maturity – Females, 5–7 years; males, 10–12 years

Skin – Smooth and cool to touch

Speed – Usually 3 to 7 miles per hour. Can go about 20 miles per hour if necessary for short stretches

Stubby beak – Rostrum

Dolphin Senses

Brain – Larger and more complex than other animals; area concerned with intelligence is smaller than in humans

Eyesight – Acute; able to adjust refraction to both air and water media

Hearing – Can hear many more frequencies than humans

Smell – Dolphins don't seem to have any. No evidence of olfactory (smell) nerves

Taste – Very sensitive; may use to detect prey and identify surrounding environment

Vocalizations – Whistles are specific to each individual; clicks are used for echolocation and communication.

Differences between Dolphins and Porpoises

Body Part	Dolphins	Porpoises
Teeth	Cone shaped	Flat or spade (shovel) shaped
Beak	About 3 inches	A small beak, or none
Dorsal fin	Curved	Hooked or triangular
Sounds	Produce sounds humans can hear	Produce sounds inaudible to humans, meaning we can't hear them
Behavior	Have less fear of humans	Shy, rarely seen at the surface

Scientific Classification of Dolphins

Dolphins belong to a sub-order of cetaceans called odontoceti. These are whales with teeth and a single blowhole. The sub-order includes orca, sperm whales, beaked whales, pilot whales, dolphins, and porpoises.

Bottlenose dolphins belong to the scientific family delphinidae.

The hippopotamus is the nearest land relative to whales and dolphins.

72

What to Do if You Find a Stranded Dolphin

Immediately contact the local police or the regional marine mammal stranding agency. Remember, dolphins are wild animals. It is illegal to touch or go closer than 100 feet from a marine mammal. Under the Marine Mammal Protection Act getting closer than 100 feet or touching a marine mammal is considered harassment and has a hefty federal fine and jail time. Dolphins carry diseases that could be transmitted to humans and vice-versa. Any small amount of bacteria or virus could cause an epidemic that could infect a whole pod.

National Stranding and Rescue networks are listed at the National Marine Fisheries web site:
nmfs.noaa.gov/pr/healthy/report.htm

In New England:
NOAA Fisheries – stranding and entanglement hotline –
1-866-755-6622
New Hampshire – Seacoast Science Center -
603-997-9448
Maine – Marine Mammals of Maine – hotline –
1-800-532-9552
Maine – College of the Atlantic – hotline –
1-800-532-9551
Massachusetts – New England Aquarium –
617-973-5247

Glossary

Beak – The forward-projecting jaws of a cetacean

Blowhole – Nostrils on the top of the heads of whales, dolphins and porpoises

Blubber – Cetaceans' insulating layer of fat

Calf – A baby cetacean. Some sources define a "calf" as a youngster still being nursed; other sources use "calf" as a general term for any young dolphin.

Cetacean – Whales, dolphins and porpoises

Crustacean – Marine creatures with exoskeleton: lobsters, crabs

Dolphin – Relatively small cetacean with conical teeth and usually a dorsal fin

Dolphin-safe tuna – Tuna that has been caught without harming dolphins. In the United States ". . . no tuna were caught on the trip . . . by a purse seine net intentionally deployed on or to encircle dolphins . . . " NOAA enforces dolphin-safe policies.

Dead zone – Coastal water containing too little oxygen to sustain life. The cause is excess nutrients, most commonly nitrogen and phosphorous, that seep into the water system from fertilizers and other chemicals. These nutrients fertilize algae blooms along the coast. The algae die and sink to the bottom where they feed bacteria. The bacteria consume dissolved oxygen from the surrounding water. This limits the oxygen available for fish and other bottom-dwelling organisms.

Dorsal fin – Large curved or hooked fin located mid-back. It functions for direction and stability.

Drift net – A large fishing net that hangs freely in the ocean, drifting with the currents. It traps birds, turtles, fish, dolphins and other marine creatures. It is illegal in the United States 200 mile coastal waters.

Ear slits – Small openings on the side of dolphins' heads; not connected to the brain

Echolocation – System used by many cetaceans to orient, navigate and find food by sending out sounds and interpreting the returning echoes.

Flipper – Another term for the pectoral fin

Flukes – Horizontally flattened tail fins. It is plural because there is a notch in the center that divides flukes into right and left sides. It is made of cartilage. It has no bones or muscles.

Gill net – Fishing net used along the shore in a fixed location, not free floating. New England fishermen have developed a small, bobber-like device called a "pinger" that attaches to the net and gives off a high pitched pinging sound to warn dolphins and other mammals.

Herd – Many pods of dolphins swimming together; may include up to 1,000 dolphins

Jetty – A solid structure built from the shore into the ocean to protect a coast or harbor from wave damage, often made of piled rocks or cement

Juvenile – young cetacean not yet sexually mature

Melon – Bulbous, rounded forehead of many toothed cetaceans believed to be used to focus sounds in echolocation

Pectoral fins – Flippers, one located on each side of the body. These function like arms in a human. They modulate speed and steer.

Pod – A coordinated group of cetaceans, also referred to as a school. The term is frequently used for a dolphin group.

Purse seine net – Huge net which can encircle a school of fish. Dolphins can be trapped. Some nets allow dolphins to escape. Freeing the dolphins is mandatory in U.S.

Seaweeds – Marine plant life composed of algae. Algae are a diverse group of non-vascular plants. They do not have true leaves, stems, roots or flowers. During photosynthesis they release a large amount of oxygen into the water. Kelps are large brown seaweeds found along temperate coastlines. Atlantic kelps may reach ten feet. There are giant kelps in the Pacific that can be 120 feet.

Protection for Dolphins

Legislation

1871 – Founding of the National Marine Fisheries Service (NMFS)

1972 – Marine Mammal Protection Act. This made it illegal to harm, touch, feed, restrain or approach marine mammals in the wild.

1973 – Convention on International Trade in Endangered Species (CITES). "APPENDIX II: Species Identified as Threatened or Likely to Become Endangered If Trade Isn't Regulated." All toothed whales are protected by CITES. Bottlenose dolphins are listed.

1976 – Magnuson–Stevens Act. This established a national program to promote domestic, commercial and recreational, fishing under sound conservation and management principles. It supports and encourages the implementation and enforcement of international fishery agreements for conservation and management of highly migratory species.

1990 – US Dolphin Protection and Consumer Protection Act legislated the "Dolphin Safe" designation for tuna. It specifies that no tuna were caught on the trip in which dolphins were seriously injured or killed by deliberately setting purse seine nets on dolphins.

1991 – Similar United Nations dolphin resolution adopted.

1992 – Founding of the Marine Mammal Health and Stranding Response Program

1996 – Sustainable Fisheries Act. This established the Office of Sustainable Fisheries, which helps to implement the requirements of the Magnuson-Stevens Act. It is part of the National Marine Fisheries Service.

1997 – International Conservation Program Act – amendment to US Marine Mammal Protection Act.

2006 – Magnuson–Stevens Reauthorization Act.

Suggestions for Further Reading

Books

Carwardine, Mark. *Whales and Dolphins.* Collins
Wild Guide; Smithsonian; 2006.

Carwardine, Mark. *Whales, Dolphins and Porpoises.*
Smithsonian Handbook, Dorling Kindersley,
2002.

Internet Sources

The Blue Ocean Society for Marine Conservation –
www.blueoceansociety.org

BlueVoice, Saving Dolphins & Whales –
www.bluevoice.org

Dolphin Research Center –
www.dolphins.org/our_mission

Earth Island Institute; International Marine Mammal
Project – www.earthisland.org/immp/

EPA Environmental Protection Agency –
www.epa.gov

The Institute for Marine Mammal Studies –
www.imms.org

10 Amazing Dolphin Superpowers – listverse.
com/2013/09/03/10-amazing-dolphin-
superpowers/

Marine Conservation Organizations –
www.MarineBio.org

National Geographic – www.animals.
nationalgeographic.com/animals/mammals/
bottlenose-dolphin/

NOAA – National Marine Fisheries Service –
www.nmfs.noaa.gov/

NOAA – National Marine Sanctuaries – sanctuaries.
noaa.gov/dolphinsmart

Ocean Conservancy – www.oceanconservancy.org

Surfrider Foundation – 60 chapters in U.S. and
International – www.surfrider.org

Wikipedia: Dolphins –
www.wikipedia.org/wiki/Dolphin

About the Author

Nancy Donovan is a writer of children's stories, a poet and a potter. Her love of nature and the environment is demonstrated in her stories that both entertain and educate. Her books, *Oscar the Herring Gull* and *Marissa the Forest Spirit* are in bookstores, toy stores and historical places on the New England seacoast. Her poems are included in three anthologies published by the Poetry Society of New Hampshire.

Nancy is a volunteer for the Odiorne Point Seacoast Science Center in Rye, New Hampshire, and a marine docent for the University of New Hampshire.

She is the mother of four great children and the grandmother of eight also wonderful kids. In her previous life, she was a nurse.

Nancy may be contacted at:
beachtreeatthec@comcast.net
More information is available at:
www.nancydonovanauthor.com

About the Illustrator

Illustrator Susan Spellman is a two-time Mom's Choice Awards® Gold Recipient, most recently for *Satchi and Little Star* (2012). She has illustrated *Highlights for Children* magazine and more than thirty children's titles. A member of the National Association of Women Artists, she has won many awards for her oil paintings. Her studio is in Newburyport, Massachusetts. More information is available at:

www.suespellmanstudio.com

Author Statement

The United States has taken a leadership role in the protection of dolphins in the wild. There are legislative restrictions on the kinds of nets used and locations. In New England, fishermen have worked to develop dolphin-safer equipment. The University of New Hampshire has developed, with fishermen, a pinger device to put on gill nets to warn away marine mammals.

However, we have not done as well with discarding/dumping toxic waste, debris, especially plastics, and fertilizers. Dead zones and plastic-filled gyres are expanding and have become ocean-wide problems.

Many other countries still continue with a slaughter of dolphins despite United Nations mandates. Dolphins do not understand territorial boundaries.

We have to separate reality from fiction. In real life, it is illegal in the United States to touch wild dolphins—both for our safety and theirs. They are wild mammals, as are bears, tigers, wolves—they are not your pet dog.

In some future time we may learn to communicate with dolphins, perhaps even form partnerships with them to protect the oceans. But we have much to learn.

We need to respect the planet.

All the water on Earth is all there ever was or will be. We can't afford to forget that.